Angels Laundromat

Short Stories *by*

Lucia Berlin

TURTLE ISLAND : Berkeley : 1981

Copyright © Lucia Berlin

ISBN 0-913666-35-1 Trade Paperback $4.95
ISBN 0-913666-3904 Trade Clothbound $10.00

Earlier versions of some of these stories first appeared in *Wild Dog, The Noble Savage, The Critic, London Strand* and *The Atlantic Monthly*. *Maggie May* first appeared under the title *Manual for Cleaning Women* in a limited chapbook edition published by *Zephryous Image Inc*. Grateful acknowledgement is made to the editors of each of these individual publications.

ANGELS LAUNDROMAT is published by Turtle Island for the Netzahaulcoyotl Historical Society, a non-profit educational corporation engaged in the multi-cultural study of New World History and Literature. For more information, address *Turtle Island, 2845 Buena Vista Way, Berkeley CA 94708.*

The illustrations for ANGELS LAUNDROMAT were drawn by MICHAEL SHANNON MOORE.

85 501006

TABLE OF CONTENTS

The Musical Vanity Boxes	9
Mama and Dad	29
El Tim	41
A Foggy Day	53
Angel's Laundromat	63
Maggie May	71

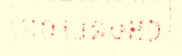

Angels Laundromat

The Musical Vanity Boxes

"Hear the instruction of thy father and mother, for they shall be an ornament of grace unto thy head and chains about thy neck. If sinners entice thee, consent not."

Mamie, my grandmother, read that over twice. I tried to remember what instruction I had had. Don't pick your nose. But I did want a chain, one that rang when I laughed, like Sammy's. . . .

I bought a chain and went to the Greyhound bus depot where a machine printed things on metal disks . . . a star in the center. I wrote LUCHA and hung it around my neck.

It was late in June, 1943, when Sammy and Jake cut Hope and me in. They were talking with Ben Padilla and at first made us go away. When Ben left Sammy called us out from under the porch.

"Sit down, we're going to cut you in on something."

60 cards. On the top of each card was a tinted picture of a Musical Vanity Box. Next to it was a red seal that said DON'T OPEN. Under the seal was one of the names on the card. Thirty 3-letter names with a line beside them. *Amy, Mae, Joe, Bea,* etc.

"It costs a nickel to buy a chance on a name. You write the person's name next to it. When all the names are sold we open the red seal. The person who chose that name wins the Vanity Box."

"Hell of a lot of Vanity Boxes!" Jake giggled.

"Shut up, Jake. I get these cards from Chicago. Each one makes a buck and a half. I send them a dollar for each and they send me the boxes. Got that?"

"Yeah," Hope said. "So?"

"So you two get a quarter for every card you sell, and we get a quarter. That makes us fifty-fifty partners."

"They can't sell all those cards," Jake said.

"Sure we can," I said. I hated Jake. Teen-age punk.

"Sure they can," Sammy said. He handed the cards to Hope. "Lucha's in charge of the money. It's eleven thirty . . . get going . . . we'll time you."

""Good luck!" they shouted. They were shoving each other over in the grass, laughing.

"They're laughing at us . . . they think we can't do it!"

We knocked on our first door . . . a lady came and put on her glasses. She bought the first name. ABE. She wrote her name and address next to it, gave us five pennies and her pencil. Precious loves, she called us.

We stopped at every house on that side of Upson.

By the time we reached the park we had sold twenty names. We sat down on the wall of the cactus garden, out of breath, triumphant.

The people thought we were darling. We were both very little for our age. Seven. If a woman answered I sold the chance. My blonde hair had grown out twice the size of my head, like a big yellow tumbleweed. "A spun gold halo!" Because my teeth were gone I put my tongue up when I smiled, as if I were shy. The ladies would pat me and bend down to hear ... "What is it, angel? Why, I'd just love to!"

If it was a man Hope sold. "Five cents ... pick a name" she drawled, handing them the card and the pencil before they could shut the door. They said she had spunk and pinched her dark bony cheeks. Her eyes glared at them through her heavy black veil of hair.

We were concerned now only with time. It was hard to tell when people were home or not. Cranking the door-bell handles, waiting. Worst of all was when we were the only visitors in 'ever so long.' All of these people were very old. Most of them must have died a few years later.

Besides the lonely people and the ones who thought we were darling, there were some ... two that day ... who really felt it was an omen to open the door and be offered a chance, a choice. They took up the most time, but we didn't mind ... waited, breathless too, while they talked to themselves. Tom? That darn Tom. Sal. My sister called me Sal. Tom. Yes, I'll take Tom. What if it wins??

We didn't even go to the houses on the other side of Upson. We sold the rest in the apartments across from the park.

One o'clock. Hope handed the card to Sammy, I poured the money onto his chest. "'Christ!" Jake said.

Sammy kissed us. We were flushed, grinning on the lawn.

"Who won?" Sammy sat up. The knees of his levis were green and wet, his elbows green from the grass.

"What does it say?" Hope couldn't read. She had flunked first grade.

ZOE

"Who?" We looked at each other . . . Which one was that?"

"It's the last one on the card."

"Oh." The man with the ointment on his hands. Psoriasis. We were disappointed, there were two really nice people we had wanted to win.

Sammy said we could keep the cards and money until we had sold them all. We took them over the fence and under the porch. I found an old breadbox to keep them in.

We took three cards and left through the alley, in back. We didn't want Sammy and Jake to think we were too eager. We crossed the street, ran from house to house, knocking on doors, all the way down the other side of Upson. All down one side of Mundy to the Sunshine Grocery.

We had sold two whole cards . . . sat on the curb drinking grape soda. Mr. Haddad kept bottles for us in the freezer, so it came out slushy . . . like melted popsickles. The buses had to make a narrow turn at the corner, just missing us, honking. Behind us the dust and smoke rose around Cristo Rey Mountain, yellow foam in the Texan afternoon sun.

I read the names aloud—over and over. We put X's

by the ones we hoped would win . . . O's by the bad ones.

The barefoot soldier . . . "I NEED a Musical Vanity Box!" Mrs. Tapia . . . "Well, come in! Good to be seeing you!" A girl sixteen, just married, who had showed us how she painted the kitchen pink, herself. Mr. Raleigh—spooky. He had called off two Great Danes, had called Hope a sexy runt.

"You know . . . we could sell a thousand names a day . . . if we had roller skates."

"Yeah, we need roller skates."

"You know what's wrong?"

"What?"

"We always say . . . 'Do you want to buy a chance?' We should say 'chances.' "

"How about . . . Want to buy a whole card?"

We laughed, happy, sitting on the curb.

"Let's sell the last one . . ."

We went around the corner, the street below Mundy. It was dark, matted with eucalyptus and fig and pomegranate trees, Mexican gardens, ferns and oleander and zinnits. The old women didn't speak English. "No, gracias," shutting the doors.

The priest from Holy Family bought two names. JOE and FAN.

There was a block then of German women, flour on their hands. They slammed the doors. Tsch!

"Let's go home . . . this isn't any good."

"No, up by Vilas school there are lots of soldiers."

She was right. The men were outside in khakis and T-shires, watering yellow bermuda grass and drinking beer. Hope sold. Her haid stuck now in strings over her olive Syrian face, like a black bead curtain.

One man gave us a quarter and his wife called him before he got his change. "Give me five!" he yelled through the screen door. I started to write his name. "No," Hope said. "We can sell them again."

Sammy opened the seals.

Mrs. Tapia had won with SUE, her daughter's name. We had an X by her, she was so nice. Mrs. Overland won the next. Neither of us could remember who she was. The third winner was a man who bought LOU which really should have gone to the soldier who gave us the quarter.

"We should give it to the soldier," I said.

Hope lifted up her hair to look at me, almost smiling ... "ok."

I jumped the fence to our yard. Mamie was watering. My mother was playing bridge, my dinner was in the oven. I read Mamie's lips over H. V. Kaltenborn news from indoors. Granpa wasn't deaf, he just turned it up loud.

"Can I water for you, Mamie?" No thanks.

I banged the front door rippling stained glass on the wall. "Git in here!" he yelled over the radio. Surprised, I ran in, smiling, started to climb into his lap but he rustled me away with a clipped out paper.

"You been with those dirty A-rabs?"

"Syrians," I said. His ashtray glowed red like the stained glass door.

That night ... Fibber McGee and Amos and Andy on the radio. I don't know why he liked them so much. He always said he hated colored people.

Mamie and I sat with the Bible in the dining room. We were still on Proverbs. "Open rebuke is better than secret love." "Why?" "Never mind." I fell asleep and she put me to bed.

I woke when my mother got home . . . lay awake beside her while she ate Cheese Tid-Bits and read a mystery. Years later, I figured out that during World War Two alone my mother ate over 950 boxes of Cheese Tid-Bits.

I wanted to talk to her, tell her about Mrs. Tapia, the guy with the dogs, how Sammy had cut us in 50-50. I put my head down on her shoulder, Cheese Tid-Bit crumbs, and fell asleep.

The next day Hope and I went first to the apartments on Yandell Avenue. Young army wives in curlers, chenille bathrobes, mad because we woke them. None of them bought a chance. "No, I *don't* have a nickel."

We took a bus to the Plaza, transferred to a Mesa bus to Kern Place. Rich people . . . landscaping, chimes on the doors. This was even better than the old ladies. Texan Junior League, tanned, bermuda shorts, lipstick and June Allyson page boys. I don't think they had ever seen children like us, children dressed in their mothers' old crepe blouses.

Children with hair like ours. While Hope's hair ran down her face like thick black tar, mine stood up and out like a tufted yellow beachball, crackling in the sun.

They always laughed when they found out what we were selling, went to find some "change." We heard one of them talking to her husband . . . "Just come and see them. Actual Urchins!" He did come, and he was the only one who bought a chance. The women just gave us money. Their children stared at us, pale, from their swing sets.

"Let's go to the depot . . ." We used to go there even before the cards . . . to hang around and watch everybody kissing and crying, to pick up dropped change beneath the ledge under the newsstand. As soon as we got in the door we poked each other, giggling. *Why* hadn't this ever occurred to us? Millions of people with nickels and nothing to do but wait. Millions of soldiers and sailors who had a girl or a wife or a child with a three-letter name.

We made out a schedule. In the mornings we went to the train station. Sailors stretched out on the wooden benches, hats folded over their eyes, like parentheses. "Huh? Oh, morning, sweethearts! Sure."
Old men sitting. Paying a nickel to talk about the other war, about some dead person with a three-letter name.
We went into the COLORED waiting room, sold three names before a white conductor pushed us out by our elbows. We spent afternoons at the USO across the street. The soldiers gave us free lunch, stale ham and cheese sandwiches wrapped in wax-paper, Cokes, Milky Ways. We played ping-pong and pin-ball machines while the soldiers filled out the cards. Once we made a quarter each punching the little counter that kept track of how many servicemen came in while the woman that did that went somewhere with a sailor.
New soldiers and sailors kept coming in with each train. The ones who were already there told them to buy our chances. They called me Heaven; and Hope, Hell.
The plan had been to keep all sixty cards until they were sold but we kept getting more and more money

and extra tip money and couldn't even count it.

We couldn't wait to see who had won anyway, even though there were only ten cards left. We took the three cigar boxes of money and the cards to Sammy.

"Seventy dollars?" Jesus Christ. They both sat up in the grass. "Crazy damn kids. They did it."

They kissed and hugged us. Jake rolled over and over, holding his stomach, squealing "Jesus . . . Sammy you are a genius, a mastermind!"

Sammy hugged us. "I knew you could do it."
He looked through all the cards, running his hand through his long hair, so black it always looked wet. He laughed at the names that had won.

PFC Octavius Oliver . . . Fort Sill, Oklahoma. "Hey, where'd you *find* these cats?" Samuel Henry Throper, Anywhere, USA. He was an old man in the COLORED part who said we could have the Vanity Box if he won.

Jake went to the Sunshine grocery and brought us drippy banana popsicles. Sammy asked us about all the names, about how we did it. . . . We told him about Kern place and the pretty housewives in chambray shirtdresses, about the USO, about the pin-ball machines, the dirty man with the Great Danes.

He gave us seventeen dollars . . . more than fifty-fifty. We didn't even take a bus, just ran downtown to Penney's. Far. We bought skates and skate keys, charm bracelets at Kress and a bag of red salted pistachio nuts. We sat by the alligators in the plaza . . . Soldiers, Mexicans, Winos.

Hope looked around. . . . "We could sell here . . ."

"No, nobody's got money here."

"But us!"

"Worst part will be delivering the Musical Vanity Boxes."

"No, because now we have skates."

"Tomorrow let's learn to skate . . . hey we can even skate down the viaduct and watch the slag at the smelter."

"If the people aren't home we can just leave them inside the screen door."

"Hotel lobbies would be a good place to sell."

We bought drippy Coney Islands and root beer floats to go. That was the end of the money. We waited to eat until we got to the vacant lot at the beginning of Upson.

The lot was on top of a walled hill, high above the sidewalk, overgrown with fuzzy grey plants that had purple blossoms. Between the plants all over the lot was broken glass dyed to different shades of lavender by the sun. At that time of day, late afternoon, the sun hit the lot at an angle so that the light seemed to come from beneath, from inside the blossoms, the amethyst stones.

Sammy and Jake were washing a car. A blue jalopy with no roof and no doors. We ran the last block, the skates thumping inside the boxes.

"Who's is it?"

"Ours, want a ride?"

"'Where'd you get it?"

They were washing the tires. "From a guy we know," Jake said. "Want a ride?"

"Sammy!"

Hope was standing up on the seat. She looked like she was crazy. I didn't understand yet.

"Sammy—where'd you get the money for this car?"

"Oh, here and there . . ." Sammy grinned at her,

drank from the hose and wiped his chin with his shirt.

"Where did you get the money?"

Hope looked like an ancient old pale yellow witch. "You cheating mother-fucker!" she screamed.

Then I understood. I followed her over the fence and under the porch.

"Lucha!" Sammy, my first hero, called, but I followed her to where she squatted by the bread-box.

She handed me the stack of filled cards. "Count them." It took a long time.

Over 500 people. We looked over the ones we had put X's by, hoping that they would win.

"We could buy Musical Vanity boxes for some of them..."

She sneered. "With what money? There is no such thing as a Musical Vanity Box anyway. You ever hear of a Musical Vanity Box before?"

She opened the bread-box and took out the ten unsold cards. She was crazy, grovelling in the dust under the porch like a dying chicken.

"What are you doing, Hope?"

Panting, she crouched in the honeysuckle opening to the yard. She held up the cards, like the fan of a mad Queen.

"They're mine now. You can come. Fifty-fifty. Or you can stay. If you come it means you are my partner and you can't ever talk to Sammy again the rest of your life or I'll murder you with a knife."

She left. I lay down in the damp dirt. I was tired. I just wanted to lie there, forever, and never do anything at all.

I lay there a long time and then I climbed over the wooden fence to the alley. Hope was sitting on the curb at the corner, her hair like a black bucket over her head. Bent, like a Pietá.

"Let's go," I said.

We walked up the hill toward Prospect. It was evening . . . all the families were outside watering the grass, murmuring from porch swings that creaked as rhythmically as the cicadas.

Hope banged a gate behind us. We walked up the wet concrete path toward the family. Iced tea, sitting on the steps, the stoop. She held out a card.

"Pick a name. Ten cents a chance."

We started out early the next morning with the rest of the cards. We said nothing about the new price, about the six we had sold the night before. Most of all we said nothing about our skates . . . for two years we'd been hoping for skates. We hadn't even tried them on yet.

When we got off the bus at the Plaza, Hope repeated that she'd kill me if I ever spoke to Sammy again.

"Never. Want Blood?" We were always cutting our wrists and sealing promises. "No."

I was relieved. I knew I would talk to him someday and without blood it wouldn't be so bad.

The Gateway Hotel, like a jungle movie. Spitoons, clicking puncas, palm trees, even a man in a white suit, fanning himself like Sidney Greenstreet. They all waved us away, rattled their faces back behind their papers as if they knew about us. People like the anonymity of hotels . . .

Outside, across the heat sinking tar of the street to catch a trolley for Juarez. Mexicans in rebozos—

smelling like American paper bags and Kress candycorn, yellow-orange.

Unfamiliar territory . . . Juarez. I knew only the fountained mirrored bars, the Cielito lindo guitar players of my mother's war-widow nights out with the "Parker girls." Hope only knew the dirty-donkey movies. Mrs. Haddad always sent her along on Darlene's dates with soldiers, so everything would be ok.

We stayed at the Juarez end of the bridge, leaning like the taxi-drivers, the wooden snake sellers against the shade of the Follies Bar, padding forward as they did when the clusters of tourists, bobbing boy-soldiers came off the bridge.

Some smiled at us, anxious to be charmed, to be charming. Too hurried and awkward to look at our cards, shoving us pennies, nickels, dimes. "Here!" We hated them, as if we had been Mexicans.

By late afternoon the soldiers and tourists squirted off the ramp, clattering onto the sidewalk into the slow hot wind of black tobacco and Carta Blanca beer, flushed, hopeful . . . what will I see? They gushed past us, pushing pennies nickels into our fists without ever looking at the upheld cards or into our eyes.

We were reeling, giddy from the nervous laughter, from the lurching out, darting out of the way. We laughed, bold now, like the wooden snake and clay pig sellers. Insolent, we stood in their way, tugging at them. "Come on, only a dime. . . . Buy a name, 10 cents. . . . Hey rich lady, a lousy dime!"

Dusk. Tired and sweaty. We leaned against the wall to count the money. The shoeshine boys watched us, mocking, even though we had made six dollars.

"Hope, let's throw the cards into the river."

"What and just beg like these sick bums?" She was furious. "No, we're going to sell every name."

"We've got to eat sometime."

"Right." She called to one of the street boys . . . "Oye, where can we eat?"

"Eat shit, gringa."

We got off the main street of Juarez. You could look back at it, hear it, smell it, like a huge polluted river.

We began to run. Hope was crying. I had never seen her cry.

We ran like goats, like colts, heads lowered clopping clopping over the mud sidewalks, loping then, muffled. Sidewalks hard red dirt.

Down some adobe steps into the Gavilán Cafe.

In El Paso, those days, 1943, you heard a lot about war. My grandfather pasted Ernie Pyle into scrapbooks all day, Mamie prayed. My mother was a Gray Lady at the hospital, played bridge with the wounded. She brought blind or one-armed soldiers home to dinner. Mamie read to me from Isaiah about how someday everybody would beat their swords into plowshares. But I hadn't thought about it. I had simply missed and glorified my father who was a lieutenant somewhere overseas . . . Okinawa. A little girl, I first thought about war when we went into the Gavilán Cafe. I don't know why, I just remember thinking then about the war.

It seemed everyone in the Gavilán Cafe was a brother, or a cousin, a relative, even though they sat apart at tables or at the bar. A man and a woman, arguing and touching. Two sisters flirting over their mother's back. Three lean brothers in denim work clothes, stooped with the same falling brother lock of hair over their tequilas.

It was dark cool and quiet although everyone was talking and someone was singing. The laughter was unstrained, private, intimate.

We sat on stools at the bar. A waitress came over, carrying a tray with a blue and purple peacock on it. Her black-rooted hennaed hair was piled into wavy mounds, caught with combs of gold and carved silver and broken mirrors. Fuchsia enlarged mouth. Green eyelids . . . a crucifix of blue and green butterfly wings sparkled between her conic yellow satin breasts. "Hola!" she smiled. Brilliance of goldcapped teeth, red gums. Dazzling Bird of Paradise!

"Qué quieren, lindas?"

"Tortillas," Hope said.

The lady-bird waitress leaned forward, dusting crumbs away with blood-red nails murmuring to us still in her green Spanish.

Hope shook her head . . . "No sé."

"Son gringas?"

"No" . . . Hope pointed to herself. Syrian. She spoke then in Syrian and the waitress listened, her fuchsia mouth moving with the words. "Eh!"

"*She's* a gringa," Hope said about me. They laughed. I envied their dark languages, their dark eyes.

"Son Gringas!" the waitress told the people in the café.

An old man came over to us, carrying his glass and a Corona beer bottle. Straight . . . standing, walking straight and Spanish in a white suit. His son followed in a black zoot-suit, dark glasses, watch chain. This was Be-Bop time, Pachuco time. . . . The son's shoulders were stooped, in fashion, head lowered to the level of his father's pride.

"What's your name?"

Hope gave him her Syrian name . . . Sha-a-hala. I gave him the name the Syrians called me . . . Luchaha. Not Lucía or Lucha but Lu-Cha-a. He told everybody our names.

The waitress was named Chata, because her nose turned up like a rain pipe. Literally, it means squat. Or bed pan. The old man was Fernando Velasquez and he shook hands with us.

Having greeted us, the people in the cafe ignored us as before, accepting us with their easy indifference. We could have leaned against any of them and fallen asleep.

Velasquez took our bowls of green chili over to a table. Chata brought us lime sodas.

He had learned English in El Paso where he worked. His son worked there too in construction. "Oye, Raúl . . . díles algo. . . . He speaks good English."

The son remained standing, elegant behind his father. His cheek bones shone amber above a bebop beard.

"What are you kids doing over here?" the father asked.

"Selling."

Hope held up the stack of cards. Fernando looked at them, turned each of them over. Hope went into her sales pitch about the Vanity Boxes . . . the name that wins gets a Musical Vanity Box . . ."

"Válgame Diós . . ." He took the card over to the next table, explained it, gesturing, banging on the table.

They all looked at the card and at us, uncertainly.

A woman in a bandana turban beckoned to me. . . . "Oye, somebody wins the boxes, no?"

"Sí."

Raúl had moved over, silent, to pick up one of the cards, looked down at me. His eyes were white through his dark glasses.

"Where are the *boxes?*"

I looked at Hope.

"Raúl . . ." I said. "Of *course* there are no Musical Vanity Boxes. The person that wins the name wins all of the *money.*"

He bowed to me, with the grace of a matador. Hope bowed her wet head and cussed in Syrian. In English she said "Why did we never think of that?" She smiled at me.

"OK, chulita . . . give me two names."

Velasquez was explaining the game to people at the tables, Chata to a group of men at the bar with strong wet backs. They shoved two tables into ours. Hope and I sat at each end. Raúl stook in back of me. Chata poured beer for everyone seated around the table, like at a banquet.

"Cuánto es?"

"Un quarter."

"No tengo . . . un peso?"

"OK."

Hope stacked the money in a pile in front of her. "Hey . . . *we* still get our quarter cut." Raúl said that was fair. Her eyes glittered under eyeshade bangs. Raúl and I wrote down the names.

The names themselves were more fun in Spanish, nobody could say them right and kept laughing. BOB.

Spilt beer. It took only three minutes to fill one card. Raúl opened the seal. Ignacio Sanchez won with TED. Bravo! Raúl said he'd made just about the same amount working all day. With a flourish, Ignacio scattered the coins and crumpled bills onto Chata's peacock tray. Cerveza!

"Wait a minute . . ." Hope took out our quarter cut.

Two peddlers had come in, pulled chairs up to the table.

"Qué pasa?"

They sat with straw baskets in their laps. "Cuánto es?"

"Un peso . . . un quarter."

"Let's make it two," Paul said. "Dos pesos, 50 cents." The new men with the baskets couldn't afford it, so everyone decided they could go for one this time since they were new. They each put in a peso on the pile. Raúl won. The men got up and left without even having a beer.

By the time we had sold out four cards everyone was drunk. None of the winners had kept their money, just bought more chances, more food, tequila now.

Most of the losers left. We all ate tamales. Chata carried the tamales in a washtub, a casserole of beans we dipped into with hot tortillaas.

Hope and I went to the outhouse behind the cafe. Stumbling, shielding the candle Chata had lent us.

Yawn . . . It makes you pensive, reflexive, to pee, like New Years.

"Hey, what Time is it?"

"Oh."

It was almost midnight. Everyone in the Gavilán cafe kissed us good-bye. Raúl took us to the bridge, holding each of our tiny hands. Gentle, like the pull of a douser's branch, drawing our bony bodies into the pachuco beat of his walk, so light, slow, swinging.

Under the bridge, on the El Paso side were the shoeshine hustlers we had seen that afternoon, standing in the muddy Rio Grande, holding up cones to catch money in, digging in the mud for it if it fell. Soldiers were throwing pennies, gum wrappers. Hope went over to the rail. "Hola, pendejos!" she hollered and threw them all our quarters. Fingers back. Laughter.

Raúl put us in a taxi and paid the driver. We waved to him out the back window, watched him walk, swinging toward the bridge. Spring onto the ramp like a deer.

Hope's father started beating her the minute she got out of the taxi, whipped her up the stairs with a belt, screaming in Syrian.

No one was home but Mamie, kneeling for my safe return. The taxi upset her more than Juarez. She never went anywhere in a taxi without a bag of black pepper in case of attack.

In bed. Pillows behind me. She brought me custard and cocoa, the food she served to the sick or the damned. Custard melted like a communion wafer in my mouth. The blood of her forgiving love I drank while she stood there, praying in a pink angel gown, at the foot of my bed. Matthew and Mark, Luke and John.

Mama and Dad

The women spoke, together, about their square stucco houses and about the houses they had had before they moved to Enid.

Esther was the only one who talked about her husband. Dad, she called him, and he called her Mama, although they had no children. He was seventy-nine, almost helpless now with asthma and ulcers. Before he got so sick he had been a car salesman. They had had a colored girl twice a week and Duncan Phyfe in the dining room. "Dad was a picture of a man, then," Esther often said, and the other women felt embarrassed.

She wasn't like the other three, with their yellowed permanents and calendars in the living room. She wore lipstick and tinted her hair, sewed bright wool dresses in winter, pastel chambrays in summer. She redid every year, painted and made slip covers and café curtains. "I have to keep busy," she said. "Keeps my mind off myself."

Evelyn and Vera, who were widows, always made a face at each other when she said this. "She's pretty full of herself as it is," Vera said.

Nellie was the only one who really liked her. Nellie respected work, effort. She and Owen had worked in their filling station every day of their married life . . . "and we mays wella died when we quit."

Owen did die, in the spring, of pneumonia. Vera and Evelyn went over after the funeral to see if they could help out any. Nellie was watching TV, as if nothing had happened at all. At the commercial Vera leaned toward Nellie.

"Maybe you'd feel better if you talked about it, Nellie. I know I did."

"No sense talkin' about it. We both knew it was comin'."

"Well, it's a shock, no matter how it comes," Evelyn said.

She and Vera stood up. Vera sighed. "It's awful hard for you . . . I know when my Edwin . . ."

Nellie lit a cigarette, the flame of the kitchen match lighting only the heavy bones of her face. "It's not hard. It didn't make any difference to what went before, and I guess it won't to what's comin' now."

Esther arrived as the two women were leaving. They only nodded at her.

"I brought over a pot of coffee, Nellie. Didn't figure you'd sleep much anyhow."

Vera and Evelyn stopped to say goodbye at the curb.

"Well, I never saw the . . ."

"Now, Vera, you know Nellie, she's not one to show her feelings."

"She could show a little decent respect."

True. They said good night at the curb.

Esther and Nellie watched Ed Sullivan and the Chevy Show. Esther, always careful about being in bad taste, did not speak, and Nellie didn't speak to her.

"Well, Dad'll be wondering where I'm at," Esther said, standing up.

Nellie stayed in her chair. "You want the coffeepot?"

"No hurry. I just make instant in the mornings."

"Think I'll have another cup. That was a good idea, Esther."

"Oh, I know you and your coffee."

Esther cried on the way home, for Nellie.

Daffodils bloomed. "Well, I'm blamed!" Dad said. He had forgotten that he had planted the bulbs. He was very happy, wanted to plant more flowers, zinnias and sweet peas and asters. He had gone outside with some seeds when he fell, in pain.

Esther rode beside him in the ambulance to the county hospital. He had had a coronary and there was a blood clot in his leg. The doctor told Esther not to worry.

When she got home, Evelyn and Vera came over with a meat loaf and a batch of tollhouse cookies. Nellie came over and made some instant coffee, to cheer her up.

"I don't know how I'll ever repay you," Esther said.

The next day she called each of them on the phone and invited them to a coffee on Saturday at ten. "She coulda just hollered out the door," Nellie giggled. But the women were pleased, and a little envious.

They arrived on Esther's porch at the same time. Nellie rang the bell.

"Well, hello, girls! Come on in!"

Esther was dressed in gold, the same color as the tablecloth. ". . . and just look at the forsythia!" "Why, Esther, it's a picture!"

There was banana bread and a pineapple upside-down ccake. "I love yellow," Esther said.

The women sat in the living room, shy, awkward, holding the cups and little napkins. When they smiled they held up spotted hands to cover their false teeth.

Esther made them all just sit still while she took the dishes into the kitchen. She put on another pot of coffee and they watched DoReMi and December Bride. They were all very tired then. At the door they told Esther again how pretty everything looked and how good the cake was.

Vera gave a coffee a few weeks later, and then Evelyn did, and then Nellie.

It was Esther's idea that they should have a coffee on the first Saturday of each month, that each of them should choose three certain months for her coffee. So we can plan ahead. She chose October and April, because of the flowers, and December, because of her little silver Christmas tree. Vera picked February and June and July—the other months she had sinus too bad. Nellie didn't care, except for November, because she made good pumpkin pies. Evelyn said that whatever the others decided was fine by her.

In the next months, marked by Saturdays, the women began to buy magazines for the table decorations and recipes; they curled their hair and put on face powder. They belched in front of each other now, teased and argued, and they began to laugh.

Dad was in the V.A. hospital for five months. His leg was fine now, but he was very weak; his asthma and ulcers had gotten much worse. They had given him many tests. At first Esther had gone twice a week to visit him. But it was so far, two buses and a walk. She admitted that she didn't like to go, didn't like to hear about the food, his digestion. She hated to walk through the ward that smelled of disinfectant and urine and dirty hair, past the rows of gaunt old men lying on their backs, staring upward. She hated to hear rustling, vomiting behind the screens, to see the sick men grinning toothless at relatives who were too hot, who didn't know what to say.

One of the doctors spoke to Esther about Dad's release. He wasn't really well, the doctor said. But he was depressed and bored and he wanted to go home. Esther would have to be very patient, would have to help him a great deal.

"Yes," she said, "although it isn't easy to care for him, alone and all, I . . ."

The doctor was in a hurry. "It won't be for long," he said.

Angry, Esther took the pen from his hand, signed the paper for Dad to come home.

An intern lifted him into the taxi. Dad couldn't hold his head up. He was thin beside Esther in the car.

She reached out her hand to him and he wept.

A few days after Dad had come home the girls came over, with cookies and cupcakes for him even though he couldn't eat them. They seemed not to notice him. Their voices were shrill and Nellie smoked. Dad began to cough, lurched up from his chair. He limped, gasping and retching, toward his room.

"Poor Esther . . . it's awful hard on you," Evelyn said. They fell silent then as Dad moaned on his creaking bed, talking to himself.

Every morning he had an egg and a glass of milk. He washed his plate and fork and glass.

He made Jell-O then, resting his body against the counter. While the Jell-O thickened he sat on a stool by the refrigerator, opening the door from time to time to check on it. When it had just begun to jell he put in bits of canned pears and some cottage cheese. Each day he made a different color of Jell-O. Sometimes he added marshmallows.

Esther helped him out onto the porch. He sat there the rest of the morning, looking out into the street, his eyes filled with a shimmering haze, like that above a fire. He had Jell-O and toast for lunch, and a cup of tea. He slept all afternoon and then he had eggs or boiled chicken, Jell-O, and tea on a tray in front of the TV.

It was Esther's turn for the coffee, the first week in October. She was going to make meringues. On the day before she washed the windows, vacuumed, polished silver and furniture. She woke early on the day of the coffee and vacuumed again. She put a brilliant orange cloth on the table, made a centerpiece with orange candles and brown autumn leaves and grasses. She felt joy when she looked at the table.

Dad woke then. She washed him and changed the elastic stocking on his blotched leg, changed the bandages on his hands and arms and neck where there were sores. He breathed in a little song while she cared for him. She dressed him in tan slacks and a new shirt. He was angry. He wanted to stay in his robe. "Shush, don't upset yourself." She put on his shoes. "Well, you're ready," she said, but he lay exhausted against the stained pillowcase, his breath howling faintly from deep in his chest, the sound of distant sirens.

"I'll bring your breakfast here."

"No." He jerked up in bed.

"You stay here. Anyhow, you'll just be in my way. I'm making meringues."

He closed his eyes. Streaks of his gray matted hair stuck in rows across the pillow. His teeth fell from the roof of his mouth.

"See. You're not fit to be up."

Esther was making pimento-and-cheese sandwiches when he came into the kitchen.

"Now, Dad, you're not fit to be up. I'll wash those."

He shook his head. He held his dishes under the faucet and put them into the drainer. "Jell-O," he whispered. She reached above her into the cupboard, slid a box of lemon Jell-O across the counter to him. She got out a bowl, opened a can of pears and a carton of cottage cheese.

"You know what I want?" he asked. "Spareribs and sauerkraut. And fudge with nuts." He turned toward her grinning. She hadn't heard. She wanted him to go away, to keep out of the kitchen while she got things ready. She wanted everything nice. He sat on the stool by the refrigerator, waiting for the Jell-O.

She put the coffee on and went to dress. Brown jersey, Coral Sand lipstick.

The coffee was boiling over. "Didn't you see it?"

"No."

"Go on. Go on, now, outside. They'll be here soon."

They waited on the porch for Esther to answer the bell. Dad nodded to them from his chair.

"Birds eating your pyracanthea berries," Nellie said to him.

"Always do, Nellie."

"How you been feelin', Dad?"

He flushed, pleased, was going to answer her, but Esther had opened the door. "Why, hello, girls! Come on in!"

"What a lovely autumn table!"

"Esther, I never saw the like of you with colors . . . a picture!"

Meringues! None of them had ever had meringues. "Did you start from scratch?"

"Mercy, no. A mix," she lied. So it would seem effortless.

They ate in silence. Snow sound of meringue. On the other side of the plate-glass window Dad coughed and spat, gasping for air. They were relieved when it was time for DoReMi. The master of ceremonies waved.

"'I like him better on his night show, where he says good night to his little boy." Vera always said that.

There was a soft thud against the window. Dad cried out; his chair scraped against the cement. He opened the front door.

He was laughing. In his bandaged hands he held a dead sparrow.

"'It saw the sky in the window. Thought it was the sky! Dad-gum, I never heard of such a thing. Flew right into it.

The women drew back from the warm bird, from the sores on Dad's hands. They turned their eyes away from the old man dangling in the doorway, from the dark stain that seeped down his pants and dripped onto the cement.

"Wonder what he thought? The end of the sky!" Dad gasped. Panting, he sank down beside Nellie on the sofa. Feathers floated onto the rug.

"Get it out of here!" Esther said.

"Here, Dad, let me have the poor thing." Nellie took the bird outside, ran with it to the basket of leaves in her yard.

"Come to your room, Dad." Esther's face was pale, her lipstick had run into little lines all around her mouth, like the stitches on a rag doll.

Her tears fell onto Dad's leg as she knelt to take off his shoes.

"My pretty party! I asked you not to bother us. And soiling your pants!"

Dad lay still while she took off his wet clothes.

"Thought it got to the end of the sky!" he whispered.

She rolled up his clothes and put them in the corner. She'd take them out later. Dad was asleep, his mouth open. She covered him.

The girls had taken their dishes into the kitchen. Nellie was washing and Evelyn and Vera were drying. Esther felt dizzy. Her voice was dry. "You didn't have to do that."

"Now, Esther, you have enough to do as it is," Evelyn said.

"Thought we'd do this up, have some more coffee and visit a bit more," Nellie said.

"Shoo, then. Go sit down and let me serve it proper."

Esther passed the coffee. "Not been much of a party," she murmured. Now Esther, they said, but they couldn't hide their sullen disappointment.

Evelyn said it was time for her nap. They were all tired, moved with difficulty toward the door.

"Your table was just lovely!"

". . . and meringues!"

"Whose is next month?"

"Mine," Nellie said, "only I'm going to pretend it's still October and make a jack-o'-lantern."

The others shook their heads. That Nellie.

For her Christmas coffee, Esther was going to have a deep blue cloth, pine needles and white candles, little white cakes and candies. Her silver tree, in the window, would be decorated with blue and silver balls. On the day before the coffee, reaching into the closet for the tree, she had a heart attack.

It had not been severe, but the doctor gave her pills and put her to bed. "Exhausted," he said, and told Dad to get someone in to help out.

When the doctor had left, Esther got out of bed and went to the closet to get her bathrobe. She was very weak, she fainted. Sobbing, Dad tried to lift her, to drag her, but she was too heavy.

He lay down beside her on the green cotton rug. He put his arm around her. She was warm, resilient like white bread; her stomach moved gently with her breath. He lay with his face against the back of her neck, pressed his mouth to the damp skin that had always smelled of Jergens lotion.

Nellie came over. She made chicken noodle soup and custard. Dad didn't go in the room when Esther woke up. He made orange Jell-O. He was sitting by the refrigerator when Nellie came in with Esther's tray.

"She's asleep . . . that'll do her more good than anything."

"Nellie . . ."

"Don't you worry, Dad. Nothing's going to keep her down." Nellie picked up the pear can. "Well, of all the fool things, lettin' this juice go to waste . . . use the juice instead of water."

"Well, I'm blamed, never thought of that."

"Don't worry now, Dad. You go in to bed."

Dad went to his room, sat on the edge of his bed. He couldn't take off his shoes. He heard Nellie put the dishes away, snap the cupboard doors. The dish drainer thumped against the shelf.

She came into the hall between the two bedrooms, stood quiet, listening. "I'm goin' on home now," she said.

When she had closed the front door, Dad got up and went into Esther's room. She was asleep. He hadn't seen her without make-up since they had been very young. She looked young now, her lined face soft and full. He sat on the bench by the dresser, watching her.

She slept until late afternoon. When she woke she didn't notice him, turned her face toward the wall, sighing. Dad tiptoed from the room.

"Mama."

She was startled, turned to him without raising herself from the bed.

"Here, Mama, I've brought you some Jell-O and toast."

She stared at him in terror. He took the plate off the tray and put it down on the bed table. He smiled at her, the tray shaking in his hands.

"'Got some water on for tea," he said.

When he came back she was sitting up, the folds of her skin like frozen laundry, stiff, distorted in her wrinkled white gown.

"Thought I'd have some too, with you." He put the spilling rattling cups down by the untouched plate of Jell-O. Stooping, he pushed the pillows up behind her back.

She took the cup he held out to her.

"Drink it now, Mama," he said.

El Tim

A nun stood in each classroom door, black robes floating into the hall with the wind. The voices of the first grade, praying, *Hail Mary, Full of Grace, the Lord is with Thee.* From across the hall, the second grade began, clear, *Hail Mary, Full of Grace.* I stopped in the center of the building, and waited for the triumphant voices of the third grade, their voices joined by the first grade, *Our Father, Who art in Heaven,* by the fourth grade, then, deep, *Hail Mary, Full of Grace.*

As the children grew older they prayed more quickly, so that gradually the voices began to blend, to merge into one sudden joyful chant . . . *In the name of the Father and of the Son and of the Holy Ghost. Amen.*

I taught Spanish in the new junior high which lay at the opposite end of the playground like a child's colored toy. Every morning, before class, I went through the grade school, to hear the prayers, but also simply to go into the building, as one would go in a church. The school had been a mission, built in 1700 by the Spaniards, built to stand alone in the desert for a long time. It was different from other old schools, whose stillness and solidity is still a shell for the children who pass through them. It had kept the peace of a mission, of a sanctuary.

The nuns laughed in the grade school, and the children laughed. The nuns were all old, not like tired old women who clutch their bags at a bus stop, but proud, loved by their God and by their children. They responded to love with tenderness, with soft laughter that was contained, guarded, behind the heavy wooden doors.

Several junior high nuns swept through the playground, checking for cigarette smoke. These nuns were young and nervous. They taught "underprivileged children," "borderline delinquents," and their thin faces were tired, sick of a blank stare. They could not use awe or love like the grade school nuns. Their recourse was impregnability, indifference to the students who were their duty and their life.

The rows of windows in the ninth grade flashed as Sister Cecilia opened them, as usual, seven minutes before the bell. I stood outside the initialed orange doors, watching my ninth-grade students as they paced back and forth in front of the wire fence, their bodies loose and supple, necks bobbing as they walked, arms and legs swaying to a beat, to a trumpet that no one else could hear.

They leaned against the wire fence, speaking in

English-Spanish-Hipster dialect, laughing soundlessly. The girls wore the navy blue uniforms of the school. Like muted birds they flirted with the boys, who cocked their plumed heads, who were brilliant in orange or yellow or turquoise pegged pants. They wore open black shirts or V-neck sweaters with nothing under them, so that their crucifixes gleamed against their smooth brown chests . . . the crucifix of the pachuco which was also tattooed on the back of their hand.

"Good morning, dear."

"Good morning, Sister." Sister Cecilia had come outside to see if the seventh grade was in line.

Sister Cecilia was the principal. She had hired me, reluctantly having to pay someone to teach, since none of the nuns spoke Spanish well enough to teach children whose language was their biggest defense.

"So, as a lay teacher," she had said, "the first one at San Marco, it may be hard for you to control the students, especially since many of them are almost as old as you. You must not make the mistake that many of my young nuns do. Do not try to be their friend. These students think in terms of power and weakness. You must keep your power . . . through aloofness, discipline, punishment, control. Spanish is an elective, give as many F's as you like. During the first three weeks you may transfer any of your pupils to my Latin class. I have had no volunteers," she smiled, "you will find this a great help."

The first month had gone well. The threat of the Latin class was an advantage; by the end of the second week I had eliminated seven students. It was a luxury to teach such a relatively small class, and a class with the lower quarter removed. My native Spanish helped a great deal. It was a surprise to them that a "gringa" could speak as well as their parents, better even than they. They were impressed that I recognized their obscene words, their slang for marijuana and police. They worked hard. Spanish was close, important to them. They behaved well, but their sullen obedience and their automatic response was an affront to me.

It was easy to keep in "control," to be strict and impersonal. Not because I believed you had to be, I didn't. It was because I was afraid.

I was afraid when they mocked words and expressions that I used and began to use them as much as I. "La Piña," they jeered, because of my hair, and soon the girls cut their hair like mine. "The idiot can't write," they whispered, when I printed on the blackboard, but they began to print all of their papers.

I was afraid because these were not yet the pachucos, the hoods that they tried hard to be, flipping a switch blade into a desk, blushing when it slipped and fell. They were not yet saying: "You can't show me nothing." They waited, with a shrug, to be shown. So what could I show them? The world I knew was no better than the one they had the courage to defy.

I watched Sister Cecelia whose strength was not, as mine, a front for their respect. The students saw her faith in the God, in the life that she had chosen; they honored it, never letting her know their tolerance for the harshness she used for control.

She couldn't laugh with them either. They laughed only in derision, only when someone revealed himself with a question, with a smile, a mistake, a fart. Always, as I silenced their mirthless laughter, I thought of the giggles, the shouts, the grade-school counterpoint of joy.

Once a week I laughed with the ninth grade. On Mondays, when suddenly there would be a banging on the flimsy metal door, an imperious BOOM BOOM BOOM that rattled the windows and echoed through the building. Always at the tremendous noise I would jump, and the class would laugh at me.

"Come in!" I called, and the knocking would stop, and we laughed, when it was only a tiny first grader. He would pad in sneakers to my desk. "Good morning," he whispered, "may I have the cafeteria list?" Then he would tiptoe away and slam the door, which was funny, too.

"Mrs. Lawrence, would you come inside for a minute?" I followed Sister Cecilia into her office and waited while she rang the bell.

"Timothy Sanchez is coming back to school." She paused, as if I should react. "He has been in the detention home, one of many times—for theft," she glanced at a letter in her hand, "and narcotics. They feel that he should finish school as quickly as possible. He is much older than his class, and according to their tests he is an exceptionally bright boy. It says here that he should be 'encouraged and challenged.' "

"Is there any particular thing you want me to do?"

"No, in fact, I can't advise you at all . . . he is quite a different problem. I thought I should mention it. His parole officer will be checking on his progress."

The next morning was Halloween, and the grade school had come in costume. I lingered to watch the witches, the hundreds of devils who trembled their morning prayers. The bell had rung when I got to the door of the ninth grade. "Sacred Heart of Mary, pray for us," they said. I stood at the door while Sister Cecilia took the roll. They rose as I entered the room, "Good morning." Their chairs scraped as they sat down.

The room became still. "El Tim!" someone whispered.

He stood in the door, silhouetted like Sister Cecilia from the skylight in the hall. He was dressed in black, his shirt open to the waist, his pants low and tight on lean hips. A gold crucifix glittered from a heavy chain. His black hair was long and straight, and it glistened as if it were wet. He was half-smiling, looking down at Sister Cecilia, his eyelashes creating jagged shadows down his gaunt cheeks. Hair fell over his eyes and he smoothed it back with long slender fingers, quick, like a bird.

I watched the awe of the class. I looked at the young girls, the pretty young girls who whispered in the rest room not of dates or love but of marriage and abortion. They were tensed, watching him, flushed and alive as I had never seen them be.

Sister Cecilia stepped into the room. "Sit here, Tim," she motioned to a seat in front of my desk. He moved across the room, his broad back stooped, neck forward, tssch-tssch, tssch-tssch, the pachuco beat. "Dig the crazy nun!" he grinned, looking at me. The class laughed. "Silence!" Sister Cecilia said. She stood beside him. "This is Mrs. Lawrence. Here is your Spanish book." He seemed not to hear her. Her beads rattled nervously.

"Button your shirt," she said. "Button your shirt!"

He moved his hands to his chest, began with one to move the button in the light, with the other to inspect the buttonhole. Violently, the nun shoved his hands away, fumbled with his shirt until it was buttoned.

"Don't know how I ever got along without you, Sister," he drawled. She left the room.

It was Tuesday, dictation. "Take out a paper and pencil." The class complied automatically. "You, too, Tim."

"Paper," he commanded quietly. Sheets of paper fought for his desk.

"Llegó el hijo," I dictated. Tim stood up and started toward the back of the room. "Pencil's broken . . ." he said. His voice was deep and hoarse, like the strange hoarseness people have when they are about to cry. He sharpened his pencil slowly, turning the sharpener so that it sounded like brushes on a drum.

"No tenían fe." Tim stopped to put his hand on a girl's hair.

"Sit down," I said.

"Cool it," he muttered. The class laughed.

He handed in a blank paper, the name "EL TIM" across the top.

From that day everything revolved around El Tim. He caught up quickly with the rest of the class. His test papers and his written exercises were always excellent. But the students responded only to his sullen insolence in class, to his refusals. His silent, unpunishable denial was reflected in everything he did. Reading aloud, conjugating on the board, discussions, all of the things that had been almost fun were now almost impossible. The boys were flippant, ashamed to get things right; the girls embarrassed, awkward in front of him.

I began to give mostly written work, private work that I could check from desk to desk. I assigned many compositions and essays, even though this was not supposed to be done in ninth-grade Spanish. It was the only thing Tim liked to do, that he worked on intently, erasing and recopying, thumbing the pages of a Spanish dictionary on his desk. His compositions were imaginative, perfect in grammar, always of impersonal things . . . a street, a tree. Instinctively I wrote comments and praise on them. Sometimes I read his papers to the class, hoping that they would be impressed, encouraged by his work. Too late I realized that it only confused them for him to be praised, that he triumphed anyway with a sneer . . . *"Pues, la tengo . . ."* I've got her pegged.

Emiterio Perez repeated everything that Tim said. Emiterio was retarded, being kept in the ninth grade until he was old enough to quit school. He passed out papers, opened windows, smiled. I had him do everything the other students did. Chuckling, he wrote endless pages of neat formless scribbles that I graded and handed back. Sometimes I would give him a B and he would be very happy. Now even he would not work. *"Para qué, hombre?"* Tim whispered to him. Emiterio would become confused, looking from Tim to me. Sometimes he would cry.

Helplessly, I watched the growing confusion of the class, the confusion that even Sister Cecilia could no longer control. There was not silence now when she entered the room, but unrest . . . a brushing of a hand over a face, an eraser tapping, flipping pages. The class waited. Always, slow and deep, would come Tim's voice. "It's cold in here, Sister, don't you think?" Sister, I got something the matter with my eye, come see." We did not move as each time, every day, automatically the nun buttoned Tim's shirt. "Everything all right?" she would ask me and leave the room.

One Monday, I glanced up and saw a small child coming toward me. I glanced at the child, and then, smiling, I glanced at Tim.

"They're getting littler every time . . . have you noticed?" he said, so only I could hear. He smiled at me. I smiled back, weak with joy, with relief. Then with a harsh scrape he shoved back his chair and walked toward the back of the room. Halfway, he paused in front of Dolores, an ugly shy little girl. Slowly he rubbed his hands over her breasts. She moaned and ran crying from the room.

"Come here!" I shouted to him. His teeth flashed.

"Make me," he said. I leaned against the desk, dizzy.

"Get out of here, go home. Don't ever come back to my class."

"Sure," he grinned. He walked past me to the door, fingers snapping as he moved . . . tsch-tsch, tsch-tsch. The class was silent.

As I was leaving to find Dolores, a rock smashed through the window, landing with shattered glass on my desk.

"What is going on!" Sister Cecilia was at the door. I couldn't get past her.

"I sent Tim home."

She was white, her bonnet shaking.

"Mrs. Lawrence, it is your duty to handle him in the classroom."

"I'm sorry, Sister, I can't do it."

"I will speak to the Mother Superior," she said. "Come to my office in the morning. Get in your seat!" she shouted at Dolores, who had come in the back door. The nun left.

"Turn to page 93," I said. "Eddie, read and translate the first paragraph."

I didn't go to the grade school the next morning. Sister Cecilia was waiting, sitting behind her desk. Outside the glass doors of the office, Tim leaned against the wall, his hands hooked in his belt.

Briefly, I told the nun what had happened the day before. Her head was bowed as I spoke.

"I hope you will find it possible to regain the respect of this boy," she said.

"I'm not going to have him in my class," I said. I stood in front of her desk, gripping the wooden edge.

"Mrs. Lawrence, we were told that this boy needed special attention, that he needed 'encouragement and challenge.'"

"Not in junior high. He is too old and too intelligent to be here."

"Well, you are going to have to learn to deal with this problem."

"Sister Cecilia, if you put Tim in my Spanish class, I will go to the Mother Superior, to his parole officer. I'll tell them what happened. I'll show them the work that my pupils did before he came and the work they have done since. I will show them Tim's work, it doesn't belong in the ninth grade." I stopped. I had been shouting.

She spoke quietly, dryly. "Mrs. Lawrence, this boy

is our responsibility. The parole board turned him over to us. He is going to remain in your class." She leaned toward me, pale. "It is our duty as teachers to control such problems, to teach in spite of them."

"Well, I can't do it."

"You are weak!" she hissed.

"Yes, I am. He has won. I can't stand what he does to the class and to me. If he comes back I resign."

She slumped back in her chair. Tired, she spoke, "Give him another chance. A week. Then you can do as you please."

"All right."

She rose and opened the door for Tim. He sat on the edge of her desk.

"Tim," she began softly, "will you prove to me, to Mrs. Lawrence and to the class that you are sorry?"

He didn't answer.

"I don't want to send you back to the detention home."

"Why not?"

"Because you are a bright boy. I want to see you learn something here, to graduate from San Marco's. I want to see you go on to high school, to . . ."

"Come on, Sister," Tim drawled. "You just want to button my shirt."

"'Shut up!" I hit him across the mouth. My hand remained white in his dark skin. He did not move. I wanted to be sick. Sister Cecilia left the room. Tim and I stood, facing each other, listening as she started the ninth grade prayers. . . . *Blessed art Thou amongst women, Blessed is the fruit of thy womb, Jesus* . . .

"How come you hit me?" Tim asked softly.

I started to answer him, to say, "Because you were

insolent and unkind," but I saw his smile of contempt and disbelief as he waited for me to say just that.

"I hit you because I was angry. About Dolores and the rock. Because I felt hurt and foolish for having trusted you."

His dark eyes searched my face. For an instant the veil was gone.

"I guess we're even then," he said.

"Yes," I said, "let's go to class."

I walked with Tim down the hall, conscious of avoiding the beat of his walk.

A Foggy Day

Downtown the Washington Market is deserted until midnight Sunday when suddenly the fruit and vegetable markets open out onto the streets, wild banners of lemons, plums, tangerines. Further down, toward Fulton Street, subtle reds and browns of potatoes, squash and yellow onions.

The buying and loading go on staccato until dawn when the last delivery truck is gone and the Greek and Syrian merchants speed off in black cars. By sunrise the market is as empty and dingy as it was before except for the smell of apples.

Lisa and Paul walked in the rain, in deserted downtown Manhattan. She talked. "It's like living in the country down here. Corn and watermelon in the summer. . . . Seasons. This is where they bring the Christmas trees for all New York. They're stacked for blocks and blocks. Forests! One night it snowed and three dogs were running wild like wolves in Dr. Zhivago. You couldn't smell cars or factories, just pine trees ..." She babbled on as she always did when she talked with him, or with dentists.

She wanted him to see it as beautiful, the city, her city. She knew he didn't. He was looking at the men eating raw yams and stolen grapefruit, or burning orange crates in rusty incinerators. Bronze K Ration 6 FOR A DOLLAR cans, green Gallo Port bottles glistened in the light of the fires, shimmered in the rain. An old man vomited into the gutter where purple fruit wrappers blurred indigo at the grate like crushed anemones.

He would find no beauty at night, during the time when fires dotted the landscape for blocks around, silhouetting the gestures of the men into drunken ritual dances. Or from her window at dawn, looking down upon a half-naked black boy, asleep on a dazzling truck-bed of limes.

It started to rain hard. They waited in the doorway of *Sahini and Sons, Artichokes* until it lessened into a drizzle, then they walked on again, wet. Slow and lanky, like they used to walk in Santa Fe, like old friends.

In Santa Fe Lisa's husband Benjamin had worked at George's restaurant, with Paul. George was a mean lesbian who dressed like a cowboy, imagined herself Gertrude Stein, and served Toklas-type food. Escargots, marrons glaceés. Benjamin played subdued jazz piano and Paul was headwaiter. They wore tuxedos. Neither of them said anything. The witty talkative patrons all dressed like Indians . . . velvet, silver, turquoise.

The men got home around two-thirty in the morning, smelling like Shrimp Aurore and cigarette smoke. Lisa cooked breakfast while they counted their tips out upon the round wooden table in the kitchen. Once Sam made ten dollars for playing "Shine on Harvest Moon" five times for a politician. The men laughed, telling her about the customers and George.

Eventually they were both fired. Paul had an actual showdown with George on dusty Canyon Road, just like in High Noon. He did look a bit like Gary Cooper. She looked like Charles Laughton in cow-boy drag and Bette Davis black lipstick. She won.

In Benjamin's case he showed up to work one night and there was a Mexican with maracas singing "Nosotros, que nos quisimos tanto . . ." Benjamin rolled his Yamaha piano out, and, with difficulty, up into the VW van.

It was a good year though. Piñon smoke, laughter. The three of them listened and listened. Miles, Coltrane, Monk. They also listened to scratchy tapes of Charles Olson, Robert Duncan, Lenny Bruce.

Paul was a poet. It seemed he didn't sleep at all. He wrote, somewhere, all morning. Benjamin slept late, practiced, played most of the afternoon, and listened to music, ear-phones on, with the seriousness of a student in a language lab.

Benjamin was a large quiet man, a kind man with a firm sense of Right and Wrong. He was fatherly and patient to Lisa, except when she exaggerated (often) which he said was tantamount to lying. He never spoke in the past or future tense.

Every night she was surprised when he made love to her. He was tender, playful and passionate, kissing her everywhere, her eyes, her breasts, her toes. She loved his strong hands on her breasts and how he would make her come with his tongue. She loved the nakedness in his hazel eyes as he entered her.

Each night she thought that it would be different in the morning between them, after what had happened, as she had felt the first time she ever had sex . . . she wouldn't look the same the next day.

After they made love he would put vaseline and white gloves on his hands and then put on a Lone Ranger sleep-shade and ear-plugs. Lisa would sit up in bed, smoking, remembering silly things that had happened that day and wishing she could wake him.

During the day she spent most of her time with Paul, reading, talking, arguing at the kitchen table. Later she imagined that it rained that whole time, because for months she and Paul read Darwin and W. H. Hudson and Thomas Hardy, by a piñon fire that also existed only in her mind.

Then there was Tony. An old Harvard friend of Benjamin's, rich and darkly handsome. He drove Lisa home from Albuquerque to Santa Fe in twenty minutes, in a Masseratti, in the rain. If other cars didn't dim their lights he would turn his completely off.

He used to take Lisa to dinner at George's, to hear Benjamin play. Benjamin played fine for his old Be-Bop friend. *Round Midnight, Scrapple from the Apple, Confirmation.*

Tony wore Italian suits with leather lapels. Paul handed them menus, silent. Tony was breaking up with his wife. He sighed, "Man . . . I hate endings . . . I only dig beginnings."

"Far out," Lisa said. "I dig endings myself."

Their eyes met over crystal glasses of Cabernet Sauvignon.

". . . and there will never, ever be another you . . ." Benjamin played. A Chet Baker tune . . .

The love affair between Lisa and Tony was inevitable, or so Tony said. Cheaply predictable, Paul said. Benjamin said nothing at all.

She was nineteen years old. Not to excuse her, just that she was at an age that needs a good talking to. She loved it when Tony said things like "We were meant for each other. Our eyebrows both grow together in the middle . . . a sign of genius."

One night when Benjamin came home she said, "Ben. I want words! I want words! I want a word with you!"

He looked at her. He took off his bow tie and the nine ruby studs from his tuxedo shirt. He took off his jacket and his shoes and sat down next to her on the rollaway bed.

"Babs," he said. (He used to call her Babs.)

He was silent then, taking off his pants and shorts and socks. He sat naked on the bed, tired, and she knew what a good man he was; and she didn't give a shit.

"I'm a man of few words," he said. He held her head in his piano playing hands.

"I love you," he said. "I love you with all my heart. Don't you know that?"

"Yes," she said and she turned over and cried herself to sleep.

It all got very passionate and painful and yes cheaply predictable. Lisa left Benjamin, taking only "Far Away and Long Ago" by W. H. Hudson. She left for Tony and romance, but Tony was "going through a lot of changes right now" so she went to live alone in a stone house in Tijeras Canyon.

Benjamin drove up to the house. She had sighed, watching him come from the window. Paul walked behind him, pale.

"Hey, Babs . . . it's time to move on. We're going to New York. Go get in the van," Benjamin said.

She stood there, trying to think. Benjamin had already climbed into the VW. Paul waited in the doorway while she gathered together her few things. She lit a cigarette and sat down.

"Christ. Go get in, will you?"

Stumbling, she followed Paul.

When they got to the house, after a silent ride, Benjamin changed into a tuxedo and went to work. He was playing with Prince Bobby Jack, at the Skyline Club. ". . . she brings me coffee in my favrit cup . . ." Good blues.

Lisa and Paul packed everything into boxes from M and B Liquors An uncanny moon toppled fluorescent over the Sandia Mountains. Ordinarily she and Paul would have rejoiced at such an event. They just witnessed it, shivering outside.

"Be a good wife to him, Lisa. He loves you, with all his heart."

Benjamin and Lisa left for New York the next morning. Paul waved good-bye and walked away toward the apple trees.

Lisa drove most of the way to New York, even through Chicago. Benjamin slept most of the way, with his eyeshade on, except when they crossed the Mississippi River. That was really beautiful, the Mississippi River.

They drove through the little town where Paul was born and saw the house and the barn. At least Lisa insisted that that must be the place. . . . She could imagine him in the green field. Tow-head kid. Red-winged blackbirds. She missed Paul a lot.

"Well, Paul," Lisa said to him on the second day of his visit to New York, in the Varick Street drizzle . . . "What did you want to talk to me about?"

"Nothing, really . . . I just didn't want to wake Benjamin (Benjamin had played a Bronx wedding the night before).

"New York was a good move," he went on to say. "I can't believe how he is playing."

"Really! Man . . . he has worked . . . six months just to get in the union . . . then strip joints, one nighters, Grossingers . . . but he's been jamming with some great musicians."

"He's had some good jazz gigs though."

"I wish you had heard him play with Buddy Tate, with all those old, old-time Count Basie cats. He was really swinging."

"He's always swinging . . . he is a fine musician."

She knew that.

"I saw Red Garland last week, at Birdland. He was standing at the bar. I said hello and he said hello back."

She was thinking about Red Garland, humming how he played "You're My Everything" when her arm brushed Paul's on Varick Street. She got so dizzy with desire for Paul she stumbled, then skipped, to get back in step. I am a wicked lady she said to herself and concentrated on the sidewalk. Step on a crack, Break your mother's back.

"Let's ride the Hoboken ferry!" she said, as pleasant as ever.

They crossed to the old ferry station. It was empty. So clearly a Saturday morning. A newsman asleep, whiskery, a TIME paper-weight clutched in his hand. A cat stretched awake on the magazine rack. Silly kittens, all grey.

It was very dark. Rain swirled soot into cracked diamond sky-lights. Paul and Lisa's footsteps echoed loud, nostalgic, like in an old empty gym, or a train station in Montana late at night during some family crisis.

The ferry was barely visible in the fog, an elegant heavy Victorian lady, skirting tugs and obtusely slow garbage barges. The ferry creaked slowly, carefully into the landing. Paul and Lisa's footsteps echoed loud again on the wooden deck. Pigeons moaned above them on the rotting roof, their irridescent oil-feathers the only colour of the morning.

The two of them were alone on the boat. They laughed, changing seats a dozen times, promenading the decks. Fog surrounded the boat.

"Paul! There's no New York! No New Jersey! Maybe we're in the English Channel!"

They stared and stared out into the fog until eerily then there were yellow box cars, red cabooses from the Jersey shore. A dream about a freight yard in North Dakota.

The ferry banged into the pilings. Gulls fluttered, then balanced again on the swaying logs.

"Come on, let's get off," he said.

"If we stay we don't have to pay."

"Lisa, why don't you ever do things right? Like why don't you buy a dust pan?"

"I hate dust pans," she said, following him off the ferry. Actually she bought them often, but threw them out by mistake.

They stook outside on the way back, leaning on the salty rail, not touching.

"'I wish you were happy," he said. "When Ben went to get you . . . it was the most courageous thing I ever saw a man do. He forgave you. It saddens me to see it made so little difference."

She wanted to be sea-sick, to tell him how ever since she'd been in New York she talked to him all day long, saved his letters to read at dusk on the roof, where the sky seemed like New Mexico.

He ran his hands through his pale hair. "I missed you, Lisa. I have really missed you."

She nodded, her head bent, tears misting the water and foam like frosted glass. Her teeth chattered.

She pointed to the WORLD sign from the WORLD-TELEGRAPH building glowing neon through the fog.

"That's the first thing I see when I open my eyes every morning. WORLD. Except backwards, of course."

Clearer now, they could see her laundry on the roof above the loft on Greenwich Street. The sooty brilliant clothes flapped against the rain black buildings around City Hall.

"Look at Diana!" she laughed.

The bronze statue of Diana rose just above her laundry, as if she were going to hurl it all into the Hudson.

"But it was you who forgave me, Paul," she said.

As the ferry approached the landing the engines shut off. Even when the ferries are crowded this is a moment of terrible silence. The water slapping against the wooden hull until the boat docks with a sullen thud and a shatter of frightened gulls.

"Paul . . ." Lisa said, but she was alone. Paul had turned. He was walking in long western strides toward the metal gate at the bow, anxious now to be getting back.

Angel's Laundromat

A tall old Indian in faded Levis and a fine Zuni belt. His hair white and long, knotted with raspberry yarn at his neck. The strange thing was that for a year or so we were always at Angel's at the same time. But not at the same times. I mean some days I'd go at seven on a Monday or maybe at six-thirty on a Friday evening and he would already be there.

Mrs. Armitage had been different, although she was old too. That was in New York at the San Juan Laundry on Fifteenth Street. Puerto Ricans. Suds overflowing onto the floor. I was a young mother then and washed diapers on Thursday mornings. She lived above me, in 4-C. One morning at the laundry she gave me a key and I took it. She said that if I didn't see her on Thursdays it meant she was dead and would I please go find her body. That was a terrible thing to ask of someone; also then I had to do my laundry on Thursdays.

She died on a Monday and I never went back to the San Juan. The super found her. I don't know how.

For months, at Angel's, the Indian and I did not speak to each other, but we sat next to each other in connected yellow plastic chairs, like at airports. They skidded in the ripped linoleum and the sound hurt your teeth.

He used to sit there sipping Jim Beam, looking at my hands. Not directly, but into the mirror across from us, above the Speed Queen washers. At first it didn't bother me. An old Indian staring at my hands through the dirty mirror, between yellowed IRONING $1.50 a DUZ. and orange Day-Glo Serenity prayers. GOD GRANT ME THE SERENITY TO ACCEPT THE THINGS I CANNOT CHANGE. But then I began to wonder if he had something about hands. It made me nervous, him watching me smoke and blow my nose, leaf through magazines years old. Lady Bird Johnson going down the rapids.

Finally he got me staring at my hands. I saw him almost grin because he caught me staring at my own hands. For the first time our eyes met in the mirror, beneath DON'T OVERLOAD THE MACHINES.

There was panic in my eyes. I looked into my own eyes and back down at my hands. Horrid age spots, two scars. Un-Indian, nervous, lonely hands. I could see children and men and gardens in my hands.

His hands that day (the day I noticed mine) were on each taut blue thigh. Most of the time they shook badly and he just let them shake in his lap, but that day he was holding them still. The effort to keep them from shaking turned his adobe knuckles white.

The only time I had spoken with Mrs. Armitage outside of the laundry was when her toilet had overflowed and was pouring down through the chandelier on my floor of the building. The lights were still burning while the water splashed rainbows through them. She gripped my arm with her cold dying hand and said, "It's a miracle, isn't it?"

His name was Tony. He was a Jicarilla Apache from up north. One day I hadn't seen him but I knew it was his fine hand on my shoulder. He gave me three dimes. I didn't understand, almost said thanks, but then I saw that he was shaky-sick and couldn't work the dryers. Sober, it's hard. You have to turn the arrow with one hand, put the dime in with the other, push down the plunger, then turn the arrow back for the next dime.

He came back later, drunk, just as his clothes were starting to fall limp and dry. He couldn't get the door open, passed out in the yellow chair. My clothes were dry, I was folding.

Angel and I got Tony back onto the floor of the pressing room. Hot. Angel is responsible for all the AA prayers and mottoes. DON'T THINK AND DON'T

DRINK. Angel put a cold wet one sock on Tony's head and knelt beside him.

"Brother, believe me . . . I've been there . . . right down there in the gutter where you are. I know just how you feel."

Tony didn't open his eyes. Anybody says he knows just how someone else feels is a fool.

Angels Laundromat is in Albuquerque, New Mexico. Fourth Street. Shabby shops and junkyards, secondhand stores with army cots, boxes of one-socks, 1940 editions of *Good Hygiene*. Grain stores and motels for lovers and drunks and old women with hennaed hair and small dogs who do their laundry at Angel's. Teenage Chicana brides go to Angel's. Towels, pink shortie nighties, bikini underpants that say *Thursday*. Their husbands wear blue overalls with names in script on the pockets. I like to wait and see the names appear in the mirror vision of the dryers. *Tino, Corky, Junior.*

Traveling people go to Angel's. Dirty mattresses, rusty high chairs tied to the roofs of dented old Buicks. Leaky oil pans, leaky canvas water bags. Leaky washing machines. The men sit in the cars, shirtless, crush Hamm's cans when they're empty.

But it's Indians who go to Angel's mostly. Pueblo Indians from San Felipe and Laguna and Sandia. Tony was the only Apache I ever met, at the laundry or anywhere else. I like to sort of cross my eyes and watch the dryers full of Indian clothes blurring the brilliiant swirling purples and oranges and reds and pinks.

I go to Angel's. I'm not sure why, it's not just the Indians. It's across town from me. Only a block away is the Campus, air-conditioned, soft rock on the Muzak.

New Yorker, Ms., and *Cosmopolitan.* Wives of graduate assistants go there and buy their kids Zero bars and Cokes. The Campus Laundry has a sign, like most laundries do, POSITIVELY NO DYEING. I drove all over town with a green bedspread until I came to Angel's with his yellow sign, YOU CAN DIE HERE ANYTIME.

I could see it wasn't turning deep purple but a darker muddy green, but I wanted to come back anyway. I liked the Indians and their laundry. The broken Coke machine and the flooded floor reminded me of New York. Puerto Ricans mopping, mopping. Their pay phone was always out of order, like Angel's. Would I have gone to find Mrs. Armitage's body on a Thursday?

"I am chief of my tribe," the Indian said. He had just been sitting there, sipping port, looking at my hands.

He told me that his wife worked cleaning houses. They had had four sons. The youngest one had committed suicide, the oldest had died in Vietnam. The other two were school bus drivers.

"You know why I like you?" he said.

"No, why?"

"Because you are a redskin." He pointed to my face in the mirror. I do have red skin, and no, I never had seen a red-skinned Indian.

He liked my name, pronounced it in Italian. *Luchía.* He had been in Italy in World War II. Sure enough there was a dog tag in with his beautiful silver and turquoise necklaces. It had a big dent in it. "A bullet?" No, he used to chew it when he got scared or horny.

Once he suggested that we go lie down in his camper and rest together.

"Eskimos say laugh together." I pointed to the lime-green Day-Glo sign, NEVER LEAVE THE MACHINES UNATTENDED. We both giggled, laughing together on our connected plastic chairs. Then we sat, quiet. No sound but the sloshy water, rhythmic as ocean waves. His Buddha hand held mine.

A train passed. He nudged me: "Great big iron horse!" and we started giggling all over again.

I have a lot of unfounded generalizations about people, like all blacks are bound to like Charlie Parker. Germans are horrible, all Indians have a weird sense of humor like my mother's. One favorite of hers is when this guy is bending down tying his shoe and another comes along and beats him up and says, "You're always tying your shoe!" The other one is when a waiter is serving and he spills beans in somebody's lap and says, "Oh, oh, I spilled the beans." Tony used to repeat these to me on slow days at the laundry.

Once he was very drunk, mean drunk, got into a fight with some Okies in the parking lot. They busted his Jim Beam bottle. Angel said he'd buy him a half-pint if he would listen to him in the pressing room. I moved my clothes from the washer to the dryer while Angel talked to Tony about One day at a time.

When Tony came out he shoved his dimes into my hand. I put his clothes into a dryer while he struggled with the Jim Beam bottle cap. Before I could sit down he hollered at me.

"I am a chief! I am a chief of the Apache tribe! Shit!"

"Shit yourself, Chief." He was just sitting there, drinking, looking at my hands in the mirror. "How come you do the Apache laundry?"

I don't know why I said that. It was a horrible thing to say. Maybe I thought he would laugh. He did, anyway.

"What tribe are you, redskin?" he said, watching my hands take out a cigarette.

"You know my first cigarette was lit by a prince? Do you believe that?"

"Sure I believe it. Want a light?"

He lit my cigarette and we smiled at each other. We were very close and then he passed out and I was alone in the mirror.

There was a young girl, not in the mirror but sitting by the window. Her hair curled in the mist, wispy Botticelli. I read all the signs. GOD GIVE ME THE COURAGE. NEW CRIB - NEVER USED - BABY DIED.

The girl put her clothes into a turquoise basket and she left. I moved my clothes to the table, checked Tony's, and put in another dime. I was alone in Angel's with Tony. I looked at my hands and eyes in the mirror. Pretty blue eyes.

Once I was on a yacht off Viña del Mar. I borrowed my first cigarette and asked the Prince Aly Khan for a light. "Enchanté," he said. He didn't have a match, actually.

I folded my laundry, and when Angel came back I went home.

I can't remember when it was that I realized I never did see that old Indian again.

Maggie May

42—PIEDMONT. Slow bus to Jack London Square. Maids and old ladies. I sat next to an old blind woman who was reading Braille, her finger gliding across the page, slow and quiet, line after line. It was soothing to watch, reading over her shoulder. The woman got off at 29th, where all the letters have fallen from the sign NATIONAL PRODUCTS BY THE BLIND except for BLIND.

29th is my stop too, but I have to go all the way downtown to cash Mrs. Jessel's check. If she pays me with a check one more time I'll quit. Besides she never has any change for carfare. Last week I went all the way to the bank with my own quarter and she had forgotten to sign the check.

She forgets everything, even her ailments. As I dust I collect them and put them on her desk. 10 a.m. NAUSEEA (sp) on a piece of paper on the mantle. DIARREEA on the drain-board. DIZZY POOR MEMORY on the kitchen stove. Mostly she forgets if she took her phenobarbital or not, or that she has already called me twice at home to ask if she did, where her ruby ring is, etc.

She follows me from room to room, saying the same things over and over. I'm going as cuckoo as she is. I keep saying I'll quit but I feel sorry for her. I'm the only person she has to talk to. Her husband is a lawyer, plays golf and has a mistress. I don't think Mrs. Jessel knows this, or remembers. Cleaning women know everything.

Cleaning women do steal. Not the things the people we work for are so nervous about. It is the superfluity that finally gets to you. We don't want the change in the little ashtrays.

Some lady at a bridge party somewhere started the rumor that to test the honesty of a cleaning woman you leave little ruse-bud ashtrays around with loose change in them, here and there. My solution to this is to always add a few pennies, even a dime.

The minute I get to work I first check out where the watches are, the rings, the gold lamé evening purses. Later when they come running in all puffy and red-faced I just coolly say "Under your pillow, behind the avocado toilet." All I really steal is sleeping pills, saving up for a rainy day.

Today I stole a bottle of Spice Islands Sesame Seeds. Mrs. Jessel rarely cooks. When she does she makes Sesame Chicken. The recipe is pasted inside the spice cupboard. Another copy is in the stamp and string drawer and another in her address book. Whenever she orders chicken, soy sauce and sherry she orders another bottle of sesame seeds. She has fifteen bottles of sesame seeds. Fourteen now.

At the bus stop I sat on the curb. Three other maids, black in white uniforms, stood above me. They are old friends, have worked on Country Club Road for years. At first we were all mad . . . the bus was two minutes early and we missed it. Shit. He knows the maids are always there, that the 42—PIEDMONT only runs once an hour.

I smoked while they compared booty. Things they took . . . nail polish, perfume, toilet paper. Things they were given . . . one-earrings, 20 hangers, torn bras.

(Advice to cleaning women: Take everything that your lady gives you and say Thank You. You can leave it on the bus, in the crack.)

To get into the conversation I showed them my bottle of Sesame Seeds. They roared with laughter. "Oh, Child! Sesame seeds?" They asked me how come I've worked for Mrs. Jessel so long, most women can't handle her for more than three times. They asked if it is true she has one hundred and forty pairs of shoes. Yes, but the bad part is that most of them are identical.

The hour passed pleasantly. We talked about all the ladies we each work for. We laughed, not without bitterness.

I'm not easily accepted by most old-time cleaning women. Hard to get cleaning jobs too, because I'm not black, am "educated." Sure as hell can't find any other jobs right now. Learned to tell the ladies right away that my alcoholic husband just died, leaving me and the four kids. I had never worked before, raising the children and all.

43—SHATTUCK-BERKELEY. The benches that say SATURATION ADVERTISING are soaking wet every morning. I asked a man for a match and he gave me the pack. SUICIDE PREVENTION. They were the dumb kind with the striker on the back. Better safe than sorry.

Across the street the woman at SPOTLESS CLEANERS was sweeping her sidewalk. The sidewalks on either side of her fluttered with litter and leaves. It is autumn now, in Oakland.

Later that afternoon, back from cleaning at Horwitz', the SPOTLESS sidewalk was covered with leaves and garbage again. I dropped my transfer on it. I always get a transfer. Sometimes I give them away, usually I just hold them.

Ter used to tease me about how I was always holding things all the time.

"Say, Maggie May, ain't nothing in this world you can hang on to. Cept me, maybe."

One night on Telegraph I woke up to feel him closing a Coor's fliptop into my palm. He was smiling down at me. Terry was a young cowboy, from Nebraska. He wouldn't go to foreign movies. I just realized it's because he couldn't read fast enough.

Whenever Ter read a book, rarely—he would rip each page off and throw it away. I would come home, to where the windows were always open or broken and the whole room would be swirling with pages, like Safeway lot pigeons.

33—BERKELEY EXPRESS. The 33 got lost! The

driver overshot the turn at SEARS for the freeway. Everybody was ringing the bell as, blushing, he made a left on 27th. We ended up stuck in a dead end. People came to their windows to see the bus. Four men got out to help him back out between the parked cars on the narrow street. Once on the freeway he drove about eighty. It was scary. We all talked together, pleased by the event.

Linda's today.

(Cleaning women: As a rule, never work for friends. Sooner or later they resent you because you know so much about them. Or else you'll no longer like them, because you do.)

But Linda and Bob are good, old friends. I feel their warmth even though they aren't there. Come and blueberry jelly on the sheets. Racing forms and cigarette cutts in the bathroom. Notes from Bob to Linda "Buy some smokes and take the car . . . dooh-dah dooh-dah." Drawings by Andrea with Love to Mom. Pizza crusts. I clean their coke mirror with Windex.

It is the only place I work that isn't spotless to begin with. It's filthy in fact. Every Wednesday I climb the stairs like Sisyphus into their living room where it always looks like they are in the middle of moving.

I don't make much money with them because I don't charge by the hour, no car-fare. No lunch for sure. I really work hard. But I sit around a lot, stay very late. I smoke and read the New York Times, porno books, How to Build a Patio Roof. Mostly I just look out the window at the house next door where we used to live. 2129½ Russell Street. I look at the tree that grows wooden pears Ter used to shoot at. The wooden fence glistens with BBs. The BEKINS sign that lit our bed at night. I miss Ter and I smoke. You can't hear the trains during the day.

40—TELEGRAPH. MILLHAVEN CONVALESCENT HOME. Four old women in wheel chairs staring filmily out into the street. Behind them, at the nurses' station, a beautiful black girl dances to "I shot the sheriff." The music is loud, even to me, but the old women can't hear it at all. Beneath them, on the sidewalk, is a crude sign. "TUMOR INSTITUTE 1:30."

The bus is late. Cars drive by. Rich people in cars never look at people on the street, at all. Poor ones always do . . . in fact it sometimes seems they're just driving around, looking at people on the street. I've done that. Poor people wait a lot. Welfare, unemployment lines, laundromats, phone booths, emergency rooms, jails, etc.

As everyone waited for the 40 we looked into the window of MILL AND ADDIE'S LAUNDRY. Mill was born in a mill in Georgia. He was laying down across five washing machines, installing a huge TV set above them. Addie made silly pantomimes for us, how the TV would never hold up. Passersby stopped to join us watching Mill. All of us were reflected in the television, like a Man on the Street show.

Down the street is a big black funeral at "Fouché's." I used to think the neon sign said "Touché," and would always imagine death in a mask, his point at my heart.

I have thirty pills now, from Jessel, Burns, McIntyre, Horwitz and Blum. These people I work for each have enough uppers or downers to put a Hell's Angel away for twenty years.

18—PARK-MONTCLAIRE. Downtown Oakland. A

drunken Indian knows me by now, always says "That's the way the ball bounces, sugar."

At Park Avenue a blue County Sheriff's bus with the windows boarded up. Inside are about twenty prisoners on their way to arraignment. The men, chained together, move sort of like a crew team in their orange jump suits. With the same comraderie, actually. It is dark inside the bus. Reflected in the window is the traffic light. Yellow WAIT WAIT. Red STOP STOP.

A long sleepy hour up into the affluent foggy Montclaire hills. Just maids on the bus. Beneath Zion Lutheran church is a big black and white sign that says WATCH OUT FOR FALLING ROCKS. Everytime I see it I laugh out loud. The other maids and the driver turn around and stare at me. It is a ritual by now. There was a time when I used to automatically cross myself when I passed a Catholic church. Maybe I stopped because people in buses always turned around and stared. I still automatically say a Hail Mary, silently, whenever I hear a siren. This is a nuisance because I live on Pill Hill in Oakland, next to three hospitals.

At the foot of Montclaire hills women in Toyotas wait for their maids to get off the bus. I always get a ride up Snake Road with Mamie and her lady who says "My don't we look pretty in that frosted wig, Mamie, and me in my tacky paint clothes." Mamie and I smoke.

Women's voices always rise two octaves when they talk to cleaning women or cats.

(Cleaning women: As for cats . . . never make friends with cats, don't let them play with the mop,

77

the rags. The ladies will get jealous. Never, however, knock cats off of chairs. On the other hand always make friends with dogs, spend five or ten minutes scratching Cherokee or Smiley when you first arrive. Remember to close the toilet seats.) Furry, jowly drips.

The Blums. This is the weirdest place I work, the only beautiful house. They are both psychiatrists. They are marriage counselors with two adopted "pre-schoolers."

(Never work in a house with "pre-schoolers." Babies are great. You can spend hours looking at them, holding them. But the older ones . . . you get shrieks, dried Cheerios, accidents hardened and walked on in the Snoopy pajama foot.)

(Never work for psychiatrists, either. You'll go crazy. I could tell Them a thing or two. . . . Elevator shoes?)

Dr. Blum, the male one, is home sick again. He has asthma, for crissake. He stands around in his bathrobe, scratching a pale hairy leg with his slipper.

Oh ho ho ho Mrs. Robinson. He has over $2000 worth of stereo equipment and five records. Simon and Garfunkle, Joni Mitchell and three Beatles.

He stands in the doorway to the kitchen, scratching the other leg now. I make sultry Mr. Clean mopswirls away from him into the breakfast nook while he asks me why I chose this particular line of work.

"I figure it's either guilt or anger," I drawl.

"When the floor dries may I make myself a cup of tea?"

"Oh, look, just go sit down. I'll bring you some tea. Sugar or honey?"

"Honey. If it isn't too much trouble. And lemon if it . . ."

"Go sit down." I take him tea.

Once I brought Natasha, four years old, a black sequined clouse. For dress up. Ms. Dr. Blum got furious and hollered that it was a sexist act. For a minute I thought she was accusing me of trying to seduce Natasha. She threw the blouse into the garbage. I retrieved it later and wear it now, sometimes, for dress-up.

(Cleaning Women: You will get a lot of liberated women. First stage is a CR group; second stage is a cleaning woman; third, divorce.)

The Blums have a lot of pills, a plethora of pills. She has uppers, he has downers. Mr. Dr. Blum has Belladonna pills. I don't know what they do but I wish it was my name.

One morning I heard him say to her, in the breakfast nook, "Let's do something spontaneous today, take the kids to go fly a kite!"

My heart went out to him. Part of me wanted to rush in like the maid in the back of Saturday Evening Post. I make great kites, know good places in Tilden for wind. There is no wind in Montclaire. The other part of me turned on the vacuum so I couldn't hear her reply. It was pouring rain outside.

The play room was a wreck. I asked Natasha if she and Todd actually played with all those toys. She told me when it was Monday she and Todd got up and dumped them, because I was coming. "Go get your brother," I said.

I had them working away when Ms. Dr. Blum came in. She lectured me about interference and how she refused to "lay any guilt or duty trips" on her children. I listened, sullen. As an afterthought she told me to defrost the refrigerator and clean it with ammonia and vanilla.

Ammonia and vanilla? It made me stop hating her. Such a simple thing. I could see she really did somehow want a homey home, didn't want guilt or duty trips on her children. Later on that day I had a glass of milk and it tasted like ammonia and vanill.

40—TELEGRAPH-BERKELEY. MILL AND ADDIE'S LAUNDRY. Addie is alone in the laundromat, washing the huge plateglass window. Behind her, on top of a washer is an enormous fish head in a plastic bag. Lazy blind eyes. A friend, Mr. Walker, brings them fish heads for soup. Addie makes immense circles of flurry white on the glass. Across the street, at Saint Luke's nursery, a child thinks she is waving at him. He waves back, making the same swooping circles. Addie stops, smiles, waves back for real. My bus comes. Up Telegraph toward Berkeley. In the window of the MAGIC WAND BEAUTY PARLOR there is an aluminum foil star connected to a fly swatter. Next door is an orthopedic shop with two supplicating hands and a leg.

Ter refused to ride buses. The people depressed him, sitting there. He liked Greyhound Stations though. We used to go to the ones in San Francisco and Oakland. Mostly Oakland, on San Pablo Avenue. Once he told me he loved me because I was like San Pablo Avenue.

He was like the Berkeley dump. I wish there was a bus to the dump. We went there when we got homesick for New Mexico. It was stark and windy and gulls soar like night hawks in the desert. You can see the sky all around you and above you. Garbage trucks thunder through dust-billowing roads. Grey dinosaurs.

I can't handle you being dead, Ter. But you know that.

It's like the time at the airport, when you were about to get on the caterpillar ramp for Albuquerque.

"Oh shit. I can't go. You'll never find the car."

"Watcha gonna do when I'm gone, Maggie?" You kept asking over and over, the other time, when you were going to London.

"I'll do macrame, punk."

"Whatcha gonna do when I'm gone, Maggie?"

"You really think I need you that bad?"

"Yes," you said. A simple Nebraska statement.

My friends say I am wallowing in self-pity and remorse. Said, I don't see anybody anymore. When I smile, my hand goes involuntarily to my mouth.

I collect sleeping pills. Once we made a pact . . . if things weren't ok by 1976 we were going to have a shoot out at the end of the Marina. You didn't trust me, said I would shoot you first and run, or shoot myself first, whatever. I'm tired of the bargain, Ter.

58—COLLEGE-ALAMEDA. Old Oakland ladies all go to Hink's department store in Berkeley. Old Berkelay ladies go to Capwell's department store in Oakland. Everyone on this bus is young and black or old and white, including the drivers. The old white ones are mean and nervous, especially around Oakland Tech High School. They're always jolting the bus to a stop hollering about smoking and radios. They lurch and stop with a bang, knocking the old white ladies into posts. The old ladies' arms bruise, instantly.

The young black drivers go fast, sailing through

yellow lights at Pleasant Valley Road. Their buses are loud and smokey but they don't lurch.

Mrs. Burke's house today. Have to quit her, too. Nothing ever changes. Nothing is ever dirty. I can't understand why I am there at all. Today I felt better. At least I understood about the 30 Lancer's Rosé Wine bottles. There were 31. Apparently yesterday was their anniversary. There were two cigarette butts in his ashtray (not just his one), one wine glass (she doesn't drink) and my new Rosé bottle. The bowling trophies had been moved, slightly. Our life together.

She taught me a lot about housekeeping. Put the toilet paper in so it comes out from under. Only open the Comet tab to three houes instead of six. Waste not, want not. Once, in a fit of rebellion, I ripped the tab completely off and spilled Comet all down the inside of the stove. A mess.

(Cleaning Women: Let them know you are thorough. The first day put all the furniture back wrong . . . five to ten inches off, or facing the wrong way. When you dust reverse the siamese cats, put the creamer to the left of the sugar. Change the toothbrushes all around.)

My masterpiece in this area was when I cleaned the top of Mrs. Burke's refrigerator. She sees everything, but if I hadn't left the flashlight on she would have missed the fact that I scoured and re-oiled the waffle iron, mended the geisha girl and washed the flashlight as well.

Doing everything wrong not only reassures them you are thorough, it gives them the chance to be assertive and a "boss." Most American women are very uncomfortable about having servants. They don't know what to DO while you are there. Mrs. Burke does things like re-check her Christmas card list and iron last year's wrapping paper. In August.

Try to work for Jews or Blacks. You get lunch. But mostly Jewish and Black women respect work, the work you do and also they are not at all ashamed of spending the entire day doing absolutely nothing. They are paying *you*, right?

The Christian Eastern Stars are another story. So they won't feel guilty always try to be doing something they never would do. Stand on the stove to clean an exploded Coca-Cola off the ceiling. Shut yourself inside the glass shower. Shove all the furniture, including the piano, against the door. They would never do that, besides they can't get in.

Thank God they always have at least one TV show that they are addicted to. I flip the vacuum on for half an hour (a soothing sound), lie down under the piano with an END-DUST rag clutched in my hand, just in case. I just lie there and hum and think. I refused to identify your body, Ter, which caused a lot of hassle. I was afraid I would hit you for what you did. Died.

Burke's piano is what I do last before I leave. Bad part about that is the only music on it is "The Marine Hymn." I always end up marching to the bus stop "From the Halls of Monte-zu-u-ma . . ."

58—COLLEGE-BERKELEY. A mean old white driver. It's raining, late, crowded, cold. Christmas is a bad time for buses. A stoned hippy girl shouted "Let me off this fuckin bus!" "Wait for the designated stop!" the driver shouted back. A fat woman, a cleaning woman, vomited down the front seat onto people's galoshes and my boot. The smell was foul and several people got off at the next stop, when she did. The driver stopped at Arco station on Alcatraz, got a hose to clean it up but of course just ran it all into the back and made things wetter. He was red-faced and furious, ran the next light, endangering us all the man next to me said.

At Oakland Tech about twenty students with radios waited behind a badly crippled man. Welfare is next door to Tech. As the man got on the bus, with much difficulty, the driver said OH JESUS *CHRIST* and the man looked surprised.

Burkes again. No changes. They have 10 digital clocks and they all have the same right time. The day I quit I'll pull all the plugs.

I finally did quit Mrs. Jessel. She kept on paying me with a check and once she called me four times in one night. I called her husband and told him I had mononucleosis. She forgot I quit, called me last night to ask if she had looked a little paler to me. I miss her.

A new lady today. A real lady.

(I never think of myself as a cleaning lady, although that's what they call you, their lady or their girl.)

Mrs. Johansen. She is Swedish and speaks English with a great deal of slang, like Filipinos.

The first thing she said to me, when she opened the door, was "HOLY MOSES!"

"Oh. Am I too early?"

"Not at all, my dear."

She took the stage. An eighty year old Glenda Jackson. I was bowled over. (See, I'm talking like her already.) Bowled over in the foyer.

In the foyer, before I even took off my coat, Ter's coat, she explained to me the event of her life.

Her husband, John, died six months ago. She had found it hard, most of all, to sleep. She started putting together picture puzzles. (She gestured toward the card table in the living room, where Jefferson's Monticello was almost finished, a gaping protozoa hole, top right.)

One night she got so stuck with her puzzle she didn't go to sleep at all. She forgot, actually forgot to sleep! Or eat to boot, matter of fact. She had supper at eight in the morning. She took a nap then, woke up at two, had breakfast at two in the afternoon and went out and bought another puzzle.

When John was alive it was Breakfast 6, Lunch 12, Dinner 6. I'll tell the cockeyed world times have changed.

"No, dear, you're not too early," she said. "'I might just pop off to bed at any moment."

I was still standing there, hot, gazing into my new lady's radiant sleepy eyes, waiting for talk of ravens.

All I had to do was wash windows and vacuum the carpet. But, before vacuuming the carpet, to find a puzzle piece. Sky with a little bit of maple. I know it is missing.

It was nice on the balcony, washing windows. Cold, but the sun was on my back. Inside she sat at her puzzle. Enraptured, but striking a pose nevertheless. She must have been very lovely.

After the windows came the task of looking for the puzzle piece. Inch by inch in the green shag carpet, cracker crumbs, rubber bands from the Chronicle. I was delighted, this was the best job I ever had. She didn't "give a hoot" if I smoked or not so I just crawled around on the floor and smoked, sliding my ashtray with me.

I found the piece, way across the room from the puzzle table. It was sky, with a little bit of maple.

"I found it!" she cried. "I knew it was missing!"

"I found it!" I cried.

Then I could vacuum, which I did as she finished the puzzle with a sigh. As I was leaving I asked her when she thought she might need me again.

"Who knows?" she said.

"Well . . . anything goes," I said, and we both laughed.

Ter, I don't want to die at all, actually.

40—TELEGRAPH. Bus stop outside the laundry. MILL AND ADDIE'S is crowded with people waiting for machines, but festive, like waiting for a table. They stand, chatting at the window drinking green cans of SPRITE. Mill and Addie mingle like genial hosts, making change. On the TV the Ohio State band plays the national anthem. Snow flurries in Michigan.

It is a cold, clear January day. Four sideburned cyclists turn up at the corner at 29th like a kite string. A Harley idles at the bus stop and some kids wave at the rasty rider from the bed of a 50 Dodge pick-up truck. I finally weep.